Before reading

Look at the book cove
Ask, "What do you thin

To build independence
at the start of this boo
back to pages 6 and 7 in and read the words again with
the child.

During reading

Offer plenty of support and praise as the child reads the story. Listen carefully and respond to events in the text.

When a **Key Word** is used for the first time, it is also shown at the bottom of the page. If the child hesitates over a word, point to the **New Key Words** box and practise reading it together. If the word is phonically decodable, you can sound out the letters and blend the sounds to read the word ("d-o-g, dog"). Praise the child for their effort, then return to the story.

Pause every few pages and ask questions to check the child's understanding of what they have read. If they begin to lose concentration, stop reading and save the page for later.

Celebrate the child's achievement and come back to the story the next day.

After reading

After reading this book, ask, "Did you enjoy the story? What did you like about it?" Encourage the child to share their opinions.

Use the comprehension questions on page 54 to check the child's understanding and recall of the text.

Ladybird

Series Consultant: Professor David Waugh
With thanks to Kulwinder Maude

LADYBIRD BOOKS

UK | USA | Canada | Ireland | Australia
India | New Zealand | South Africa

Ladybird Books is part of the Penguin Random House group of companies
whose addresses can be found at global.penguinrandomhouse.com.
www.penguin.co.uk   www.puffin.co.uk   www.ladybird.co.uk

Original edition of Key Words with Peter and Jane first published by Ladybird Books Ltd 1964
Series updated 2023
This book first published 2023
001

Text copyright © Ladybird Books Ltd, 1964, 2023
Illustrations by Gustavo Mazali
Illustrations copyright © Ladybird Books Ltd, 2023

With thanks to Liz Pemberton for her contributions in advising on the illustrations
With thanks to Inclusive Minds for connecting us with their Inclusion Ambassador network,
and in particular thanks to Guntaas Kaur Chugh for her input on the illustrations

Printed in China

The authorized representative in the EEA is Penguin Random House Ireland,
Morrison Chambers, 32 Nassau Street, Dublin D02 YH68

A CIP catalogue record for this book is available from the British Library

ISBN: 978-0-241-51092-6

All correspondence to:
Ladybird Books
Penguin Random House Children's
One Embassy Gardens, 8 Viaduct Gardens, London SW11 7BW

Key Words

with Peter and Jane

7b

Keeping cool

Based on the original
Key Words with Peter and Jane
reading scheme and research by William Murray

Original edition written by William Murray
This edition written by James Clements
Illustrated by Gustavo Mazali

Peter was looking out of his window.

His sister walked in and looked out of the window with him.

The sun was out.

"It will be really hot soon," Peter said.

"I know," said Jane.

New Key Words

    window   sister   really
        soon   know

"Shall we ask Mum and Dad to take us to a museum in the city?" asked Jane.

"It might get really hot in the city. Shall we go to the park?" said Peter.

New Key Words

ask   take   museum   city   park

Peter and Jane looked at their street out of the other window.

"It's Nish and Naz from school!" said Jane.

They saw the brother and sister walking up the street to the park. Their dad was with them.

"Let's ask to go to the park with Nish and Naz," said Peter.

New Key Words

their   street   other
saw   brother

The children saw Dad having something to eat.

"Can we take our ball to the park, as it's so hot?" Peter asked him.

"Yes, but it might be more fun to go to the river," said Dad.

New Key Words

something   eat   as   so

more   river

"I do want to go to the river again," said Jane. "But we saw Nish and Naz, a brother and sister we know from school, walking to the park."

"It might be more fun at the park," said Peter.

"I know," said Mum. "How about you go to the river after the park?"

"That's a really good plan," said Dad.

New Key Words

      again   how   about

"Can we go to the cafe in the park for a drink, Dad?" asked Jane.

"And something to eat?" asked her brother.

"Yes, we can go to the park cafe," Dad said.

New Key Words

cafe   drink

Peter and Jane walked with their dad up the street.

Their dog, Tess, was with them. Tess was pleased about going to the park.

At the top of their street, they saw the park.

New Key Words

top

At the top of the park, Peter and Jane saw Nish and Naz, and other children from school. Soon, more children from their street joined them.

They all played with the ball. Peter's team had the ball more than Jane's, but Jane was the top player in the game.

Tess was playing near them. Dad sat at the cafe with a drink.

New Key Words

Jane kicked the ball really hard.

Peter kicked the ball really hard.

Tess was hot now. She walked to Dad at the cafe and had a drink of water.

Peter and Jane had something to drink and eat at the park cafe.

After that, they played with the ball again.

New Key Words

now

Jane kicked the ball really hard again. The other children saw the ball hit the top of the cafe and fall into the pond!

"How will we get our ball now?" Nish asked his sister, Naz.

New Key Words

Soon, a boy in a boat was there to help.

"I saw their ball go in. Can I do something?" the boy asked.

"Yes. Thank you for helping us," said Nish and Naz's dad.

"Who wants to get in?" the boy asked.

"Me!" said Peter.

New Key Words

who

The other children saw the boat rock as Peter hopped in.

"Don't fall in, Peter! Don't get wet!" said Dad.

Peter slid to the top of the boat. Now it rocked a bit more!

Peter grabbed the ball.

The others clapped as Peter handed Naz and her brother their ball.

New Key Words

Peter, Jane and Dad walked home from the park.

"Let's get a train to the river now," said Jane.

"We must take something from home to eat and drink," said Dad.

"And our red boat!" said Peter.

New Key Words

Peter, Jane and Dad walked to the train station. They hopped on a train to go to the river.

"I saw a picture of a city museum out of the window," Jane said to her brother.

"Can we go to the city soon, Dad?" asked Peter.

"Yes," said Dad. "We will go soon."

New Key Words

picture

Peter and Jane walked near the river with Dad.

"The river runs from the top of the hill to the city," said Dad.

Peter and Jane dropped their red boat into the river.

"Who will catch it as it floats down the river?" asked Dad.

New Key Words

Their boat was really quick on the river.

"It's stuck on something!" said Peter.

"Who knows how to get the boat from the river now?" asked Dad.

"I know how to do it," said Jane. "I can get the boat from the river."

New Key Words

With Dad's help, Jane stepped on to a log to get their boat.

"Don't fall, Jane. You don't want to get wet in the river," said Dad. "Here, take this."

Dad passed Jane a stick to get their boat.

"Get the boat, Jane!" said Peter to his sister.

Soon, they had their boat again.

New Key Words

39

Peter and Jane walked to the other riverbank.

"Now, don't fall in the river," said Dad. "You really don't want to get wet."

"Can you take a picture now, Dad?" asked Jane. "This is really good fun!"

"Yes, I'll take a picture of you on top of the rocks," he said.

New Key Words

41

As Dad walked to a good spot to take the picture, he fell into the river!

"Don't fall in the river, Dad!" said Peter and Jane. "Don't get wet!"

Dad was now really wet!

New Key Words

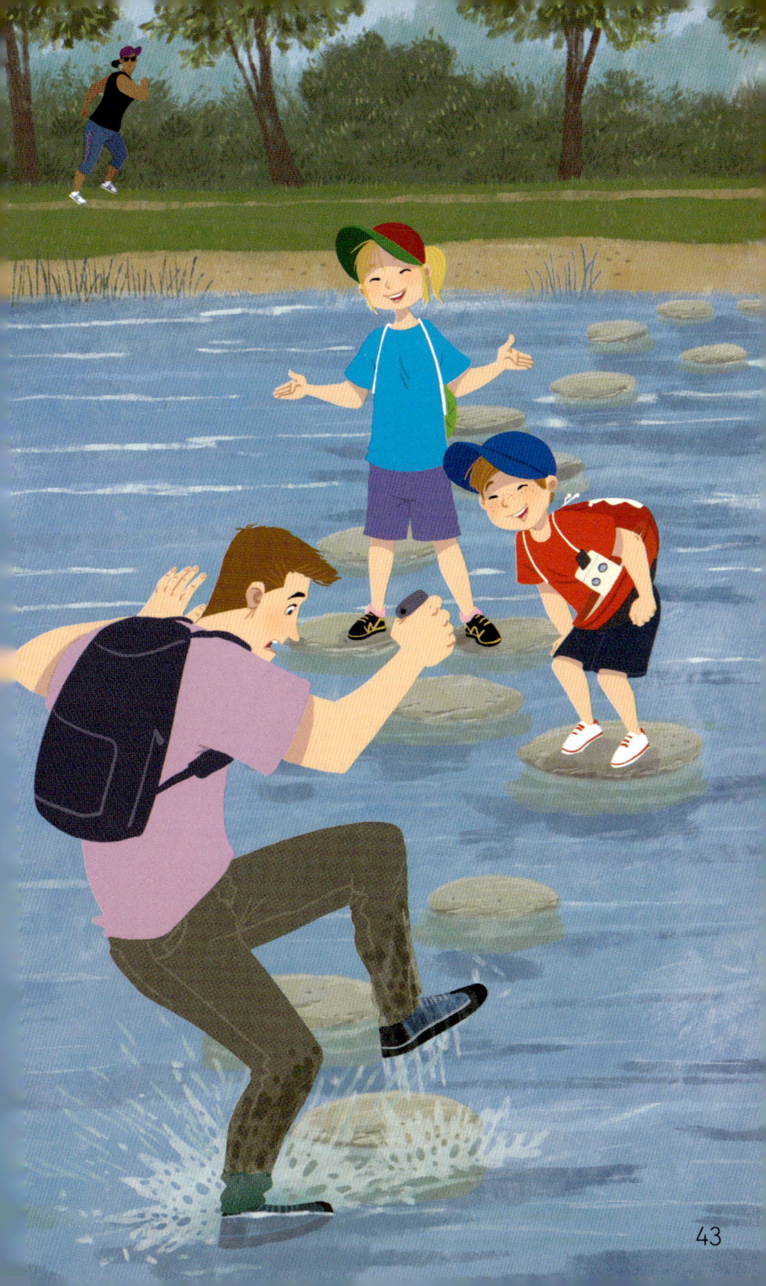

"Who wants to go home now?" asked Dad.

Dad really wanted to put on something that was not wet.

They walked to the train station again. The sun was hot, and soon Dad was less wet.

New Key Words

45

"That was really good fun," said Peter.

"Let's go on a trip to the museum in the city soon," said Dad.
"It might not be as wet!"

Peter and Jane looked at the museum picture.

"Yes, please!" they said.

New Key Words

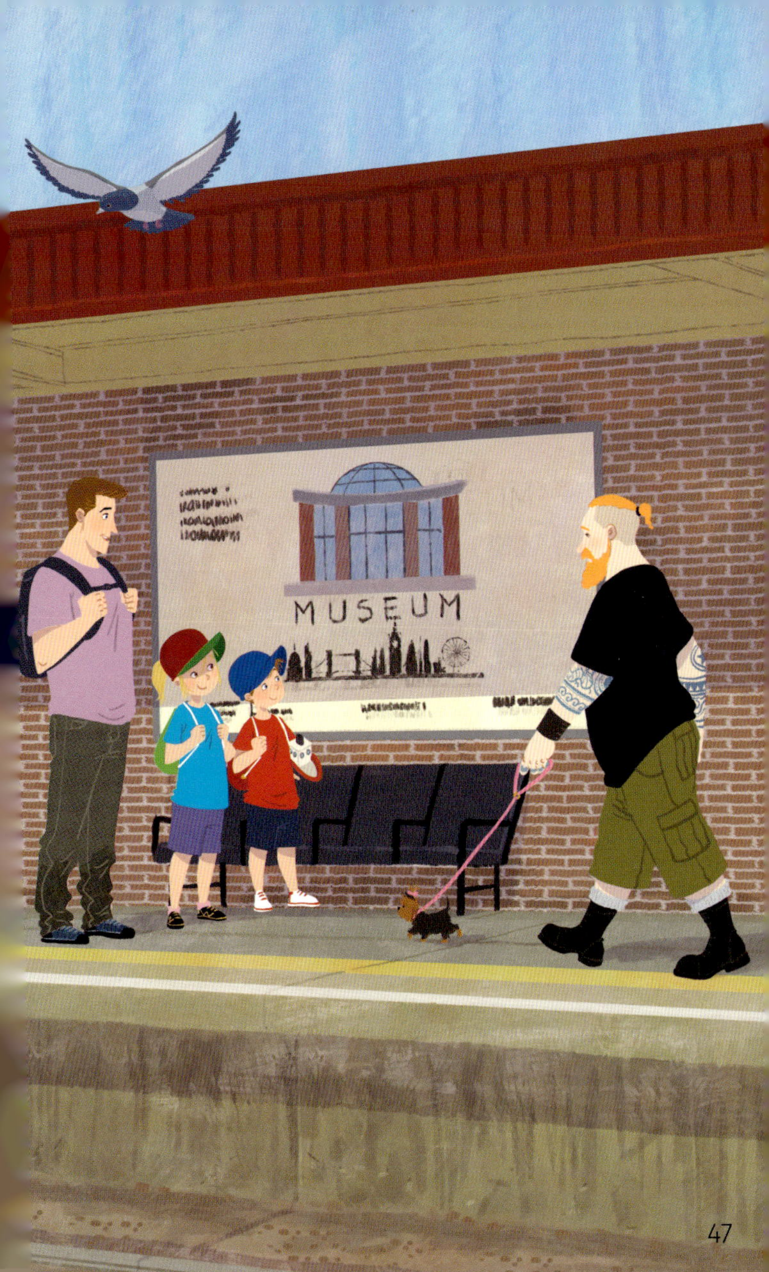
MUSEUM

They walked down their street again.

At home, Mum asked, "How was the trip to the river?"

"Really good! But do you know who fell into the river?" Jane asked.

"It was Dad!" said Peter. "We saw Dad fall into the river."

New Key Words

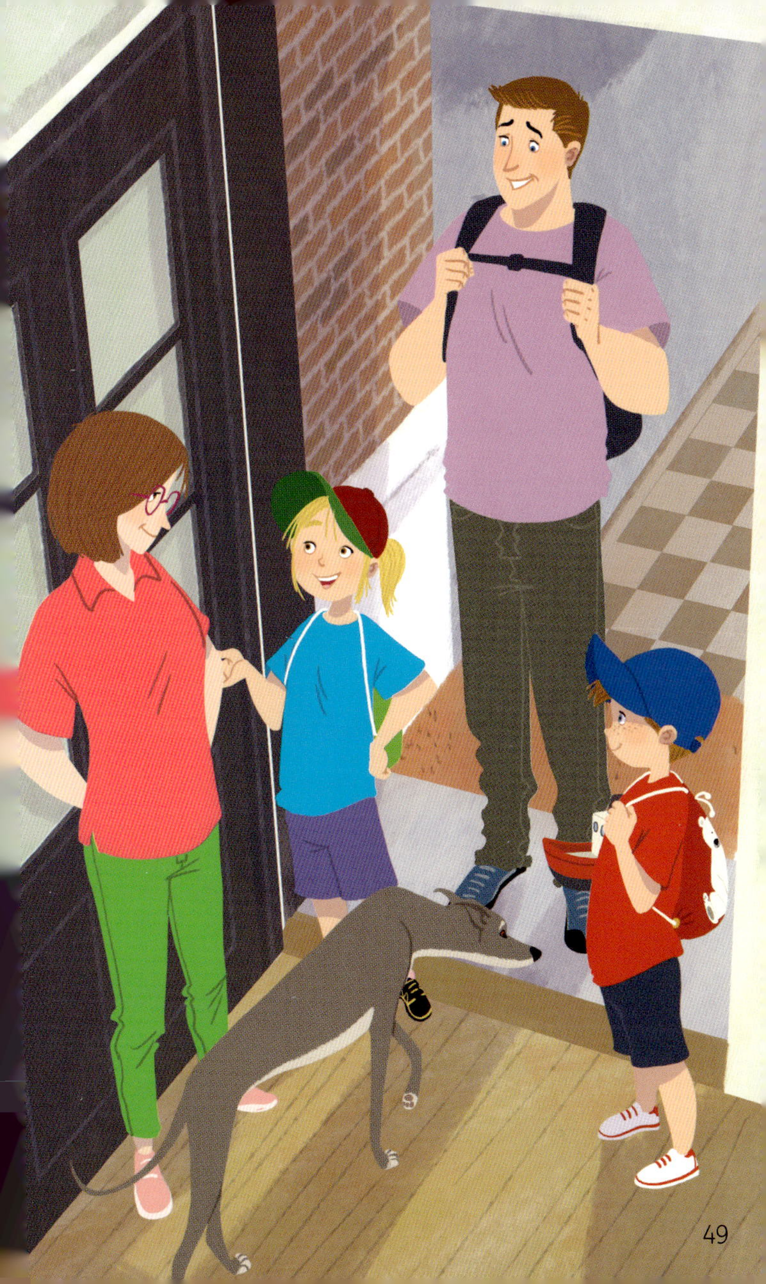

"I want to hear all about it! How about something really cold to drink?" asked Mum.

"Yes, please, and can we have ice cream to eat?" asked Jane.

Mum nodded.

New Key Words

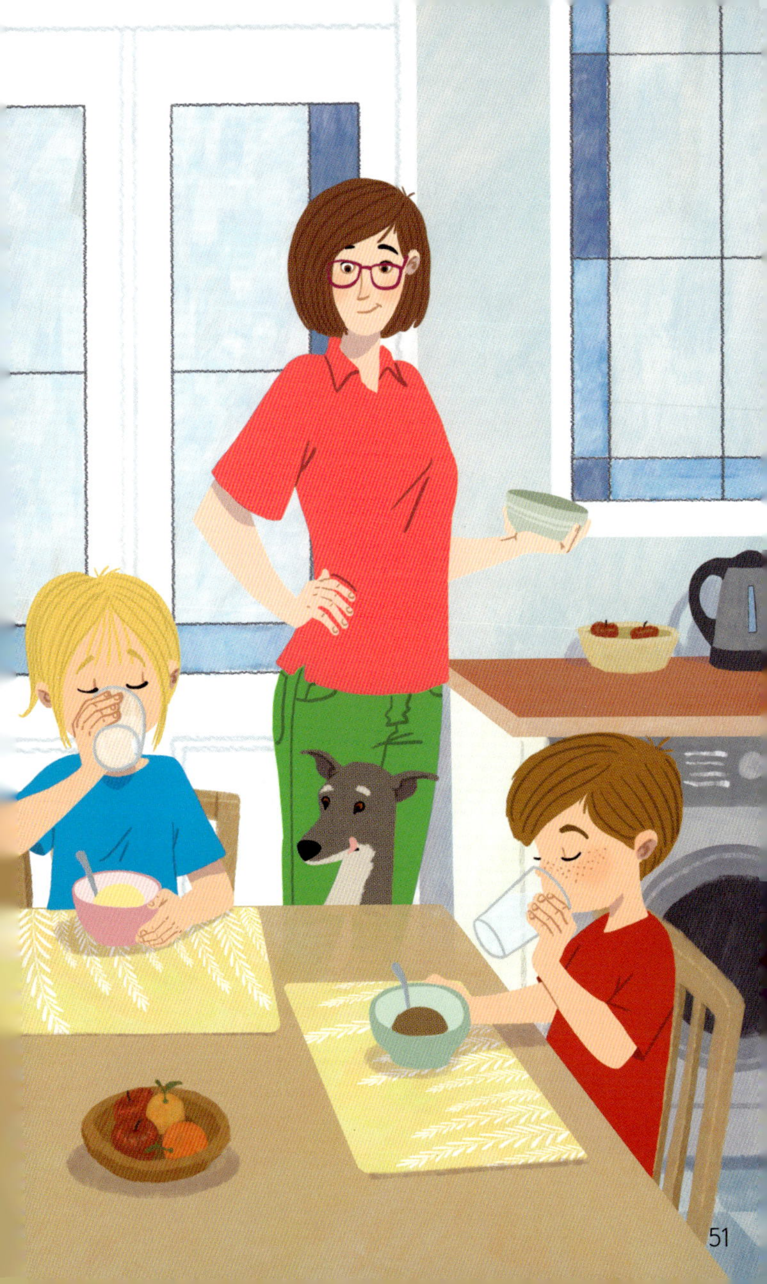

Mum had something fun to show them.

"I know you will all like this! Who wants to get in?" asked Mum.

"Not me!" said Dad. "I don't want to get wet again so soon!"

New Key Words

53

Questions

Answer these questions about the story.

1 Which school friends do Peter and Jane see out of the window?

2 Which animal plays near the children at the park?

3 Who helps the children to get the ball out of the pond?

4 What do Jane and Peter take with them to the river?

5 Who falls in the river at the end of the story? How does it happen?